TIME TO ROAR

Olivia A. Cole

illustrated by Jessica Gibson

BLOOMSBURY
CHILDREN'S BOOKS

NEW YORK LONDON OXFORD NEW DELHI SYDNEY

BLOOMSBURY CHILDREN'S BOOKS
Bloomsbury Publishing Inc., part of Bloomsbury Publishing Plc
1385 Broadway, New York, NY 10018

BLOOMSBURY, BLOOMSBURY CHILDREN'S BOOKS, and the Diana logo are trademarks of Bloomsbury Publishing Plc

First published in the United States of America in September 2020 by Bloomsbury Children's Books

Bloomsbury books may be purchased for business or promotional use. For information on bulk purchases please contact Macmillan Corporate and Premium Sales Department at specialmarkets@macmillan.com

Library of Congress Cataloging-in-Publication Data
available upon request
ISBN 978-1-5476-0370-1 (hardcover) • ISBN 978-1-5476-0371-8 (e-book) • ISBN 978-1-5476-0372-5 (e-PDF)

Artwork created in Adobe Photoshop and with a Wacom Cintiq 16
Typeset in Amasis MT Std
Book design by Danielle Ceccolini
Printed in China by Leo Paper Products, Heshan, Guangdong
2 4 6 8 10 9 7 5 3 1

All papers used by Bloomsbury Publishing Plc are natural, recyclable products made from wood grown in well-managed forests.
The manufacturing processes conform to the environmental regulations of the country of origin.

To find out more about our authors and books visit www.bloomsbury.com and sign up for our newsletters.

For my Baby Owl, who inspired this book with
her voice. May you always, always roar.
—O. A. C.

To my wonderful, supportive family.
You guys mean everything to me on this journey.
—J. G.

Every animal has a place where they feel at peace, and for Sasha, it was the meadow at the heart of the forest.

Each morning before the sun rose, the smell of green was like a song she knew by heart. She would sit in the dark and quiet and enjoy the feeling of being a bear.

But one morning, it was not dark.
It was not quiet.

Sasha stood on the hill as great yellow beasts
tore into the meadow. Silver teeth slashed at the trees
and metal feet shook the earth.

"They will keep cutting," a squirrel said sadly.
"And then the forest will be no more."

"I must save the meadow," Sasha said, and she started down the hill toward the yellow beasts.

But the squirrel stopped her. "Don't go roaring," he said. "We should call the animals together and discuss what is to be done."

Sasha knew her roar was mighty, but maybe the squirrel was right.

He climbed a tree and chattered the song
that all animals know.

The animals came out, one by one.

When they had gathered, the squirrel began to speak. "Machines have come to our forest. What can be done?"

"I will stop them," Sasha growled.

"No, no," said the bluebird. "Let me sing to them sweetly. That will make them think twice."

The bluebird winged down to the meadow, chirping a pleasant tune. He flew in loops around the machines.

But the metal clamor drowned out the sweetness.

The crashing of trees made Sasha tremble.

Next, the rabbit hopped forward. "I will thump my foot against the ground and distract them," the rabbit said.

The rabbit hopped down to the meadow,
where blades cut through clover.

The rabbit raised her strong back foot and
thumped hard.

But the ground was already quaking beneath the machines and no one heard.

This time the deer jumped up.

"I will stop them," said the deer. "I will be fast and lead them away from our forest."

But when the deer leapt into the meadow, the yellow beasts only rolled on and on, tearing up the grass and soil.

"We must hide!" the squirrel said.
"It is the only way we will survive!"

Sasha gazed down as the forest around them became more broken. Soon her meadow wouldn't be a meadow at all.

Inside her, anger welled up, sparkling. Maybe it was stronger than yellow beasts.

She lumbered down the hill to the meadow. She thought
of the ways the other animals had tried to save the forest.
She knew what had to be done.

It wasn't sweet. It wasn't a distraction. It wasn't running.
It wasn't hiding. Sometimes a bear had to raise her voice.

Sasha **ROARED**.

Then she **ROARED** again.

She **ROARED** until the yellow beasts shook.

She filled the meadow with her bellow.

When Sasha stopped, the world was very still.

And then the ground began to quiver . . .
this time as the yellow beasts fled.

Sasha stood alone in the meadow. The ground was torn from the teeth of the machines, but shook no more. She knew clover would grow again one day.

The other animals came out from the forest.

"Singing sweetly did not work," chirped the bluebird.

"I could not distract them," said the rabbit.

"Running did not lead them away," said the deer.

"I was wrong," said the squirrel. "And hiding was not the answer."

Sasha smiled at the setting sun. Soon the grass would glimmer with dew.

"You weren't wrong, friends," Sasha said. "Sometimes you must sing sweetly. Sometimes you must run and distract. And sometimes you must hide to survive."

"But sometimes," she said, settling herself on the ridge with a happy sigh, "you must be a bear. Sometimes you must ROAR."

E
Cole, Olivia A.
Time to roar

SEP - - 2020